Classroom Book Wish

Mrs Raymer
A Gift For

Grace Sullivan
From

Scholastic Book Fairs

MICHAEL LIND

Bluebonnet Girl

illustrated by KATE KIESLER

Henry Holt and Company · New York

To my mother, Marcia Hearon Lind, who devoted
her life to teaching children, and to the memory
of my grandmother, Eloise Amelia Rose Hearon,
a student of folklore and flowers —M. L.

To my family —K. K.

Henry Holt and Company, LLC, *Publishers since 1866*
115 West 18th Street, New York, New York 10011
www.henryholt.com

Henry Holt is a registered trademark of Henry Holt and Company, LLC
Text copyright © 2003 by Michael Lind. Illustrations copyright © 2003 by Kate Kiesler
All rights reserved. Distributed in Canada by H. B. Fenn and Company Ltd.
Library of Congress Cataloging-in-Publication Data
Lind, Michael. Bluebonnet girl / Michael Lind; illustrated by Kate Kiesler.
1. Comanche Indians—Folklore. I. Kiesler, Kate. II. Title.
E99.C85 L56 2002   398.2'089'9745—dc21   2001005206
ISBN 0-8050-6573-3 / First Edition—2003 / Designed by Donna Mark
Printed in the United States of America on acid-free paper. ∞
10 9 8 7 6 5 4 3 2 1

The artist used acrylic paint to create the illustrations for this book.

Come every spring
the bluebonnets cling
    to prairies the showers renew.
The brush of the rain
makes the bluebonnets stain
    the land with their very own hue.

Come every spring
the bluebonnets cling
    to prairies the showers renew.
Come, gather near,
settle down, and you'll hear
    of how the first bluebonnets grew.

Long ago, the People dwelled
amid the prairie grass.
They camped wherever drifting herds
of buffalo would mass.
The roving bison would provide
their meat and roof them with its hide.
Content, the People lived their lives
and watched the seasons pass.

But then one summer brought a drought.
    The buffalo dispersed.
The People, like the beasts and birds,
    grew thin and weak with thirst.
The People prayed, and wondered why
the spirits made the world so dry.
Was all this meant to punish them?
    Why had they been so cursed?

One old warrior, who was called
　　Spirit Talker, went alone
where the rattler shook and crawled
　　through the maze of bison bone.
To the north he turned. He raised
　　up the pipe, as he addressed
spirits of the earth. He faced
　　north and south and east and west.
What old Spirit Talker learned
　　all were told, when he returned.

"This is the message the spirits
　　gave to me on the heights.
This is the answer they gave me
　　for praying three days and three nights.

"My People, the drought that afflicts us
is punishing us for our greed.
Too long, in the plentiful seasons,
we've taken much more than we need.

"Whatever you own that you treasure,
what you will not trade for a price,
that you must toss in the campfire,
that you must sacrifice."

The warrior named Little Bison thought:
　　"Why should I sacrifice my bird-bone vest?
No other like it can be made or bought.
　　When others act, then I will join the rest.
But I won't be the first to try this test."

Beside him, River Crane was looking down.
    The moccasins she held made neighbors stare
at all their lovely beadwork. With a frown,
    she thought: "Give up my shoes? It isn't fair!
A gift like that would be more than my share."

Returning Wolf had been foremost
    among the People, in peace or in war.
Of three wives and eight children he could boast.
        His tepees looked the tallest, from afar;
        his dogs would win, when all the dogs would spar.
More than the others in the crowd,
he had good reason to be proud.

Above all else, he loved his leather shield.
        This was the prize Returning Wolf had fetched.
To him a mystic vision had revealed
        the floating eagle he had neatly sketched
        upon the shield. Its curving rim was fletched
with eagle feathers and a claw
like those worn by the bird he saw.

Now everyone belonging to the band
        was looking at Returning Wolf to learn
if he would give his shield to save the land.
He raised his trophy up, as though he planned
        to hurl it down and watch the leather burn.
Instead, he sank his shield and head
and walked away from those he led.

The People, one by one,
    departed from the fire.
No offering was made
    to feed the waning pyre.

One took away a lance;
    another took a bow.
One took away a shell,
    and one an eagle's toe.

One walked home with a rock,
    one went home with a sled.
One took a cradle-board,
    departing with bowed head.

Soon Spirit Talker stood
alone beside the flame.
Then he, too, took his pipe
and stole away in shame.

Across the west,
the sun, a red
confusion, spread.
The shadows pressed
together till
the camp was still.
No dog barked.
No firewood sparked.

Deep in the bluish night,
a solemn little girl
pushed back a tepee's curl.
The stars were crowded tight
as wood grains overhead.
The fire was nearly dead.
As tilting cinders blotched,
the girl knelt down and watched.

She clutched a doll of hide and wood
that wore a bonnet, a soft hood
of blue jay feathers. Night and day,
in sleep, at meals, in naps and play,
the doll had kept her company.
No greater offering could there be.

A dry wind rustled through a grassy tuft.
The doll was lowered, till its feathered cap
was resting on an ember. Soon it puffed.
The fire awoke. A sizzle and a snap.
The feathers on the bonnet, bright and blue,
caught fire. Away into the night they flew.

Rubbing her eyes—they stung and itched
with more than soot—the little girl
sat and watched the fragments whirl
on spiral waves of heat. Unstitched
by golden threads, the doll decayed
to cubes of coal. The girl-child prayed.

Mothlike, the flakes took flight
when she stirred an ember.
The soot was soft and light
as snowflakes in December,
a blizzard in a drought.
The pulsing ash burned out.

The child at last
stood up and passed
across the camp.
The tent was damp.
She crawled inside
the cone of hide.
The camp was still.
No embers popped.
No cinders dropped.
The camp was still.

The rains returned with crack and flash.
    Lightning split the skies.
The buffalo mistook the splash
    of pelting drops for flies.
The herds of skittish pronghorns passed,
spooked by every glow and blast.

On rippling wings the hawk careened
    over the stormlit plain
to safety under boughs that screened
    its refuge from the rain.
Coyote trotted anxiously,
tickled by what he could not see.

From flooded tunnels, prairie dogs
    emerged with baffled barks.
In creek beds, mud-encrusted frogs
    used branches as their arks.
The nightmare melted in a dream,
the drought dissolved in sparkling steam.

The morning glowed. The child awoke
to hear the folk
exclaiming all around. The girl
stretched to unfurl
the tepee flap. Outside, she saw
what caused their awe.

Blue as the slant of an afternoon squall,
blue as an ox-bow lagoon—above all,
blue as the feathers that burned on the doll—
　　bluebonnets wavered.

Voiceless with wonder, the girl stood among
stems on which blue and white blossoms were hung.
Noiseless, the bells of the flowers were rung
    by breezes they flavored.

The girl felt a hand on her shoulder.
    "I know of the price that you paid,"
Spirit Talker told her.
    "I witnessed the gift that you made.

"Because you gave up what was precious
    above all else to you,
the showers have come to refresh us
    with flowers that make the world new."

And still every spring
come the showers that bring
    bluebonnets to prairies again.
And where they appear,
it is said, you can hear
    the laugh of a child in the wind.

Author's Note

The bluebonnet, one of the most splendid flowers of
the North American prairie, is the state flower of Texas. The
name derives from the resemblance of each tiny flower to
an old-fashioned lady's bonnet. The bluebonnet and other
lupines belong to the plant family *Lupinus*, a name that
derives from the Latin word for wolf. The name originated
in the mistaken belief that the bluebonnet and other "wolf-
flowers" stole nutrients from the soil and left it depleted.

The story of the bluebonnet's origins first appeared in print in
1924 in "An Indian Legend of the Bluebonnet" by Mrs. Bruce Reid in
Legends of Texas, edited by the great folklorist J. Frank Dobie. Dobie
himself retold the legend in "The Texas Bluebonnet" in his book *Tales
of Old-Time Texas* (1928). Since then, this tale has been retold by many
authors in many versions.

In this version, the First Americans of the story are identified with
the Comanches. The members of the Comanche nation call themselves
the *Numunuh*, "The People"; the name Comanche is a Spanish version
of a Ute Indian word, *Komantcia*, which means "enemy." The Comanche
nation, part of the Shoshone group of First Americans, lived on the
northern plains of the present-day United States until the fifteenth and
sixteenth centuries C.E. In the seventeenth century, the Comanches
acquired horses, which Europeans had introduced to North America.
The Comanches quickly became skilled at hunting buffalo and fighting
on horseback. They migrated to the Southern Plains region, which
includes central and northern Texas, eastern New Mexico, and
Oklahoma. Here they came into conflict with the governments and
inhabitants of Mexico, the Republic of Texas, and the United States.
Today many members of the Comanche nation live in Oklahoma and
in other states including Texas, New Mexico, and California.